THE SILLY GOOSES

By DAV Pilkey

THE BLUE SKY PRESS

An Imprint of Scholastic Inc. • New York

For Don "Fonzie" Libertowski

THE BLUE SKY PRESS

Copyright © 1997 by Dav Pilkey

For information regarding permission, please write to:
Permissions Department,
The Blue Sky Press, an imprint of Scholastic Inc.,
555 Broadway, New York, New York 10012.
The Blue Sky Press is a registered trademark of Scholastic Inc.
Library of Congress catalog card number: 96-52916
ISBN 0-590-94733-8
10 9 8 7 6 5 4 3 2 1   8 9/9 0/0 01 02 03
Printed in Mexico   49
First printing, February 1998
The illustrations in this book were done with pencil, gouache,
acrylics, India ink, watercolors, and orange-flavored Gatorade.
Designed by Dav Pilkey and Kathleen Westray

Chapters

Chapter 1
The Silly Goose

Once upon a pond,
there lived a flock of geese.
Most of the geese were
proper and serious,
but one goose was not.

His name was Mr. Goose,
and he was very silly.
He wore silly hats,
he sang silly songs,
and he did lots and lots
of silly things.

"You had better stop
being so silly,"
the other geese warned.
"Or you will never find a wife!"

But Mr. Goose
kept right on being silly.

Soon it came time for all
of the geese to get married,
but nobody wanted
to marry Mr. Goose.

But Mr. Goose kept right on
being silly.

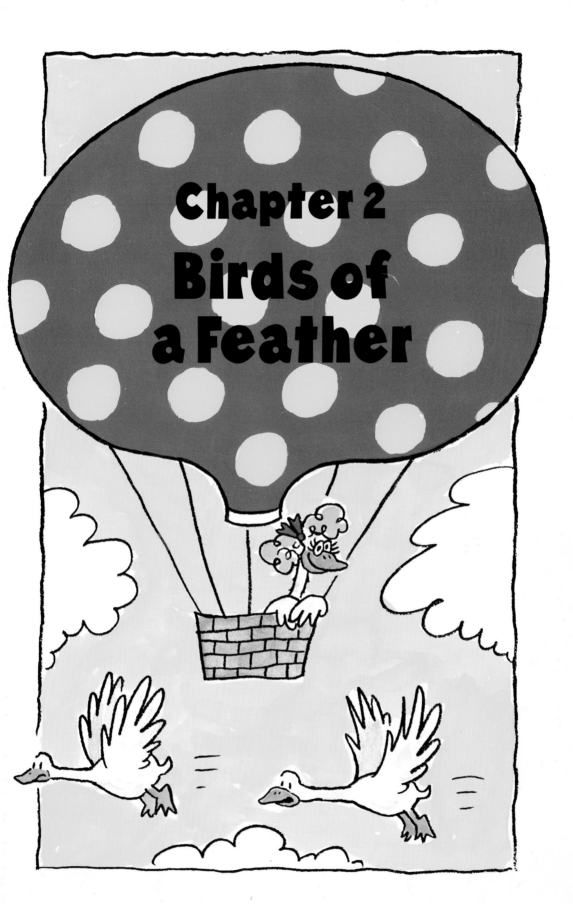

One day the geese
at the pond were sitting
in their nests.
Mr. Goose was sitting
in his bean-bag chair.

They saw a flock of geese
flying in the sky.
Most of these geese were
proper and serious, too.
But *one* goose was very silly.

"You had better stop being so silly,"
called the flying geese.
"Or you will fall out of that balloon!"

"I will not fall out,"
said the silly goose in the balloon.
"Not unless I climb over the side
and let go—like this."

Suddenly the silly goose fell out
of the balloon. Down she went.

SPLASH!

When Mr. Goose met
the other silly goose,
it was love at first sight.

"You have the most beautiful eyes,"
said Mr. Goose.
"Blub blub blubble blub blub,"
said the other silly goose.

Chapter 3
The Silly Wedding

The two silly geese
decided to get married.
Mr. Goose put on
a beautiful wedding dress.

His bride put on
a handsome tuxedo.
"My hat fits great!"
she said.

Then they ran to the chapel.
"Do you? Do you?"
asked the church mouse.
"We do! We do!"
said the silly geese.

"Hooray!" said the church mouse.
"You're married!"

After the wedding, Mr. and Mrs. Goose
were very happy.

They wanted to have a cake
and throw a big party.
But they got mixed up.

And instead, they had a party
and threw a big cake.

"Would you like to start a family?"
asked Mr. Goose.
"No," said Mrs. Goose.
"I want to have children instead."
"That's a good idea," said Mr. Goose.

So Mr. and Mrs. Goose settled into
their bright orange bean-bag chair.
A few days later, Mrs. Goose
laid two eggs.
"Look," said Mrs. Goose. "Triplets!"

Mr. Goose was so proud that
he swam out to tell all the other geese.
"I'm going to be a mother!"
he shouted.

"We can't take it!" they cried,
and they all flew south for the winter.
"But it's only June!" shouted Mr. Goose.

Chapter 5

Silly Babies

The Silly Gooses sat on their eggs
for weeks and weeks.

Finally, the big day came.
"SNAP," went one egg.
"CRACKLE," went the other egg,
and finally the two eggs popped open.

When the two Silly Goose babies
opened their eyes,
they couldn't see a thing.
"We're blind!" they cried.

"Oh, dear! Oh, dear!"
cried Mr. and Mrs. Goose,
and they rushed their babies
straight to the dentist.

"I don't know much about eyes,"
said the dentist.
"But maybe you should take
these shells off their heads.
Maybe that will help."

So the Silly Gooses took the shells
off their babies' heads.
"We can see!" cried the baby Gooses.
"Hooray!" shouted Mr. and Mrs. Goose.

The Silly Goose family was
so happy that they all went out
for ice-cream sundaes.
"We want more ketchup and
mustard on our ice cream!"
said the Silly Goose babies.

Suddenly, Mr. and Mrs. Goose
thought of two great names
for their babies. "We will call
them 'Ketchup' and 'Mustard',"
they said.

And they did.

When they had finished their ice cream,
the Silly Gooses ordered hamburgers
for dessert.
"And don't forget the hot fudge!"
said Mr. Goose.

Then, when their tummies were full, the Silly Gooses rowed a boat back to the pond. "We sure have had a silly day," said Ketchup and Mustard. "Will the rest of our days be silly, too?"

And they were.